NOBODY LIKES A
BOOGER

Written by Angela Halgrimson
Illustrated by Brian Barber

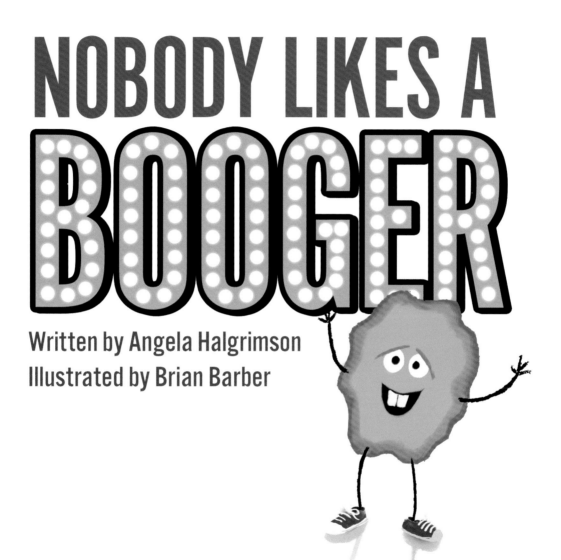

Edited by Lily Coyle
ISBN 13: 978-1-59298-824-2
Library of Congress Catalog Number: 2017907376
Printed in Canada
First Printing: 2017
21 20 19 18 17   5 4 3 2 1
Illustrations, cover, and interior design by Brian Barber

Beaver's Pond Press, Inc.
7108 Ohms Lane
Edina, MN 55439-2129
(952) 829-8818
www.BeaversPondPress.com
To order, visit www.ItascaBooks.com or call (800) 901-3480. Reseller discounts available.

To the Big Boogers that inspired the book,
Josh, Blake, and Jake. I love you.
                                    -A.H.

To my dear, cherished family and friends,
wash your hands, I don't want your cold.
                                    -B.B.

This book belongs to:

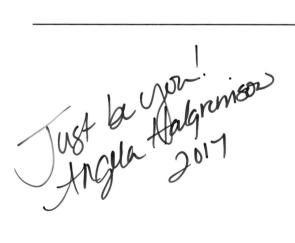

Just be you!
Angela Aalgrimson
2017

Nobody likes a booger!
How can that be?

Not even a **cute** little booger
like me!

I'm here when you're sick,
even though you yell "ICK!!"

And whenever you **cry**, I peek to see why.

But nobody likes me here or there.

Not on a table.

Not under a chair.

Nobody likes me near or far.

Not on a swing.

Or a monkey bar.

Not on a finger chasing girls.

Not on a bus.   **Not** on a train.

Not even on a superfast jet plane!

Not on the handle of
your best friend's bike.

And not on your neighbor's dog, Spike.

Nobody likes this sad, sad booger.

You will?

Then put me in my happy place, if I can't stay on your face!

A tissue

is the place to be,
for a cute little booger
like me!